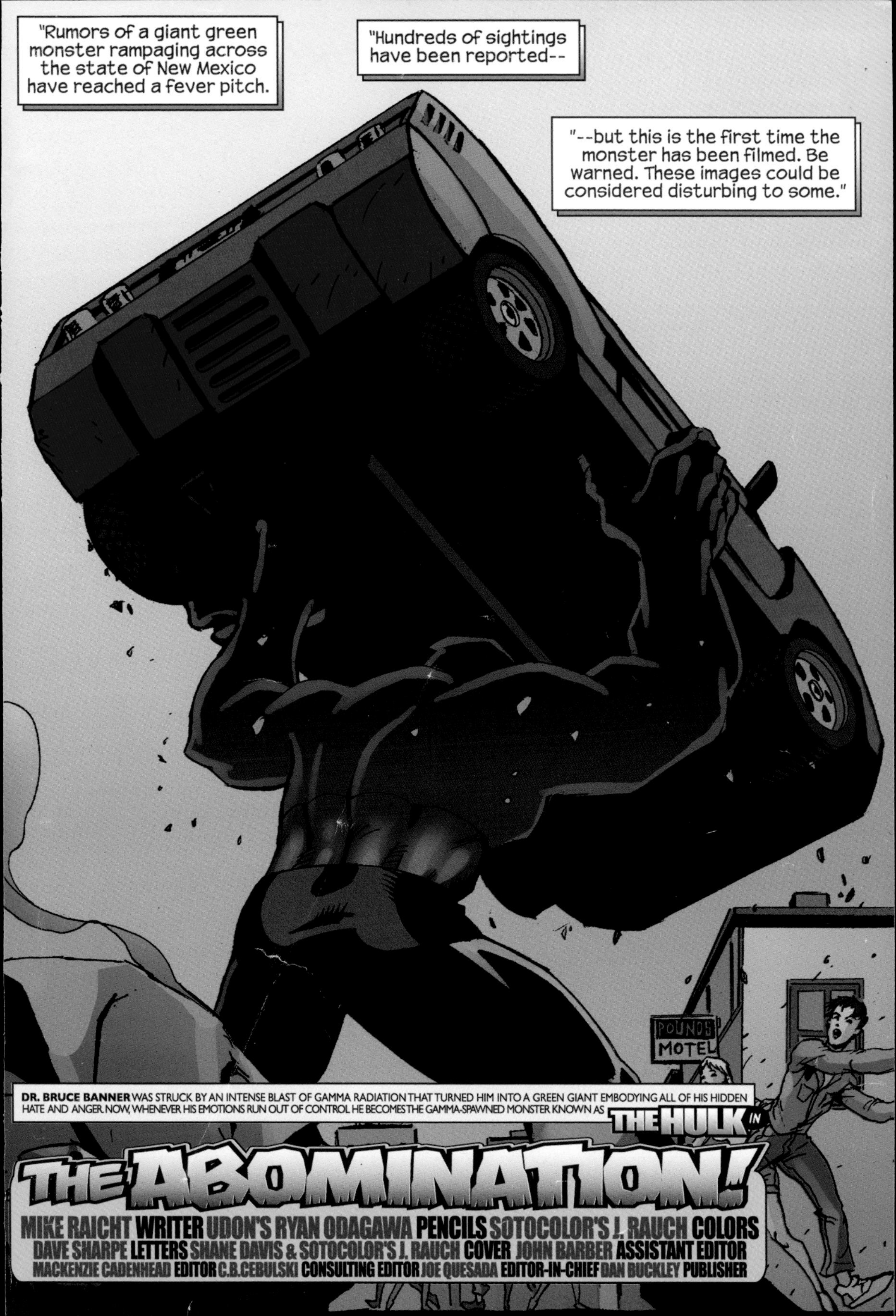
"Rumors of a giant green monster rampaging across the state of New Mexico have reached a fever pitch.
"Hundreds of sightings have been reported--
"--but this is the first time the monster has been filmed. Be warned. These images could be considered disturbing to some."
POUNDS MOTEL
DR. BRUCE BANNER WAS STRUCK BY AN INTENSE BLAST OF GAMMA RADIATION THAT TURNED HIM INTO A GREEN GIANT EMBODYING ALL OF HIS HIDDEN HATE AND ANGER. NOW, WHENEVER HIS EMOTIONS RUN OUT OF CONTROL HE BECOMES THE GAMMA-SPAWNED MONSTER KNOWN AS THE HULK IN
THE ABOMINATION!
MIKE RAICHT WRITER UDON'S RYAN ODAGAWA PENCILS SOTOCOLOR'S J. RAUCH COLORS
DAVE SHARPE LETTERS SHANE DAVIS & SOTOCOLOR'S J. RAUCH COVER JOHN BARBER ASSISTANT EDITOR
MACKENZIE CADENHEAD EDITOR C.B.CEBULSKI CONSULTING EDITOR JOE QUESADA EDITOR-IN-CHIEF DAN BUCKLEY PUBLISHER

VISIT US AT
www.abdopub.com

Spotlight, a division of ABDO Publishing Company Inc., is the school and library distributor of the Marvel Entertainment books.

Library bound edition © 2006

Library of Congress Cataloging-in-Publication Data

Raicht, Mike.
    The Hulk in The abomination! / Mike Raicht, writer ; Ryan Udagawa, pencils ; J. Rauch, colors ; Dave Sharpe, letters ; Shane Davis & J. Rauch, cover.
        p. cm.
    "Marvel age"—Cover.
    Revision of a Dec. 2004 issue of Incredible Hulk.
    ISBN 1-59961-045-0
    1. Graphic novels. I. Title: Abomination. II. Udagawa, Ryan. III. Incredible Hulk (New York, N.Y. : 1999) IV. Title.

PN6728.H8R35 2006
741.5'973—dc22

                                                    2005057557

All Spotlight books are reinforced library binding
and manufactured in the United States of America

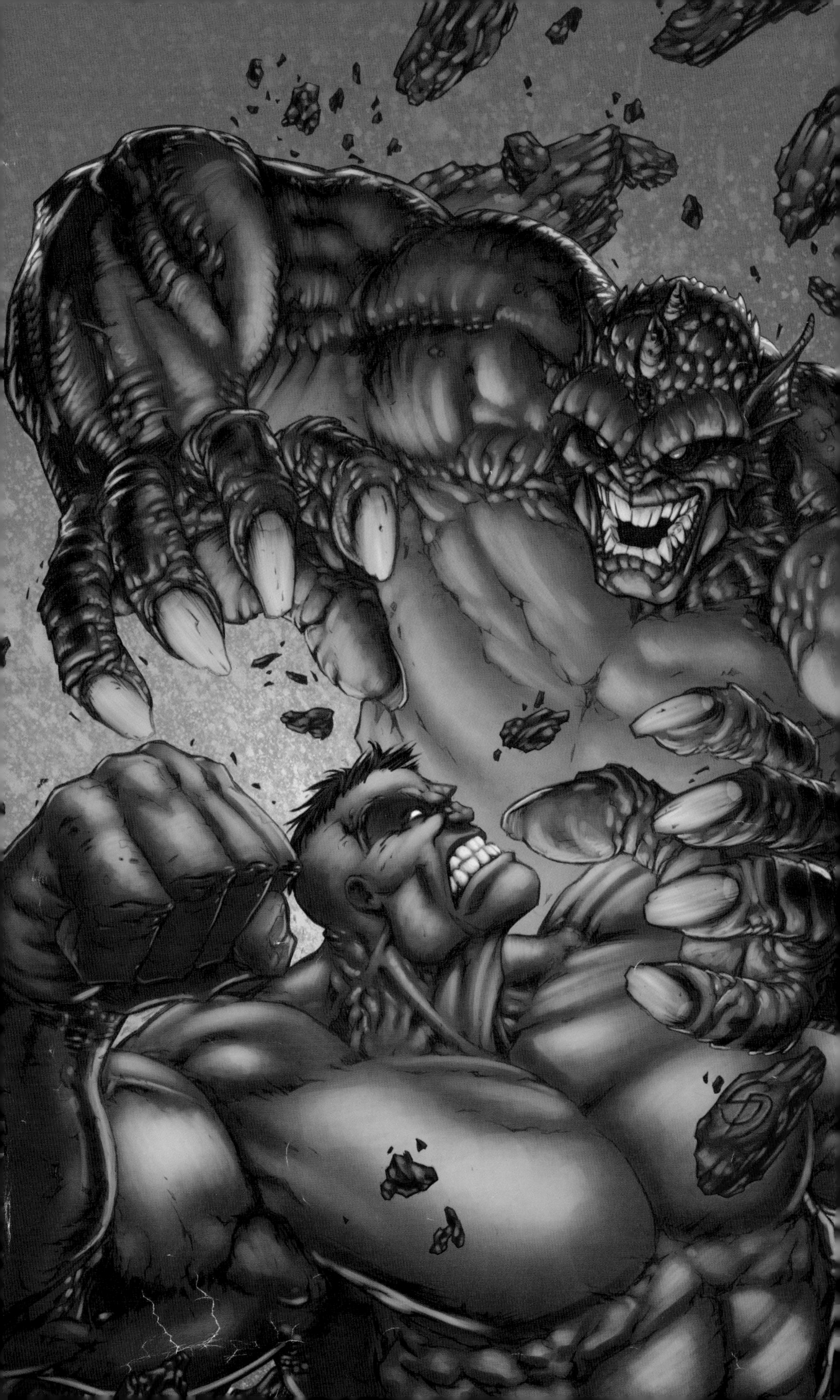

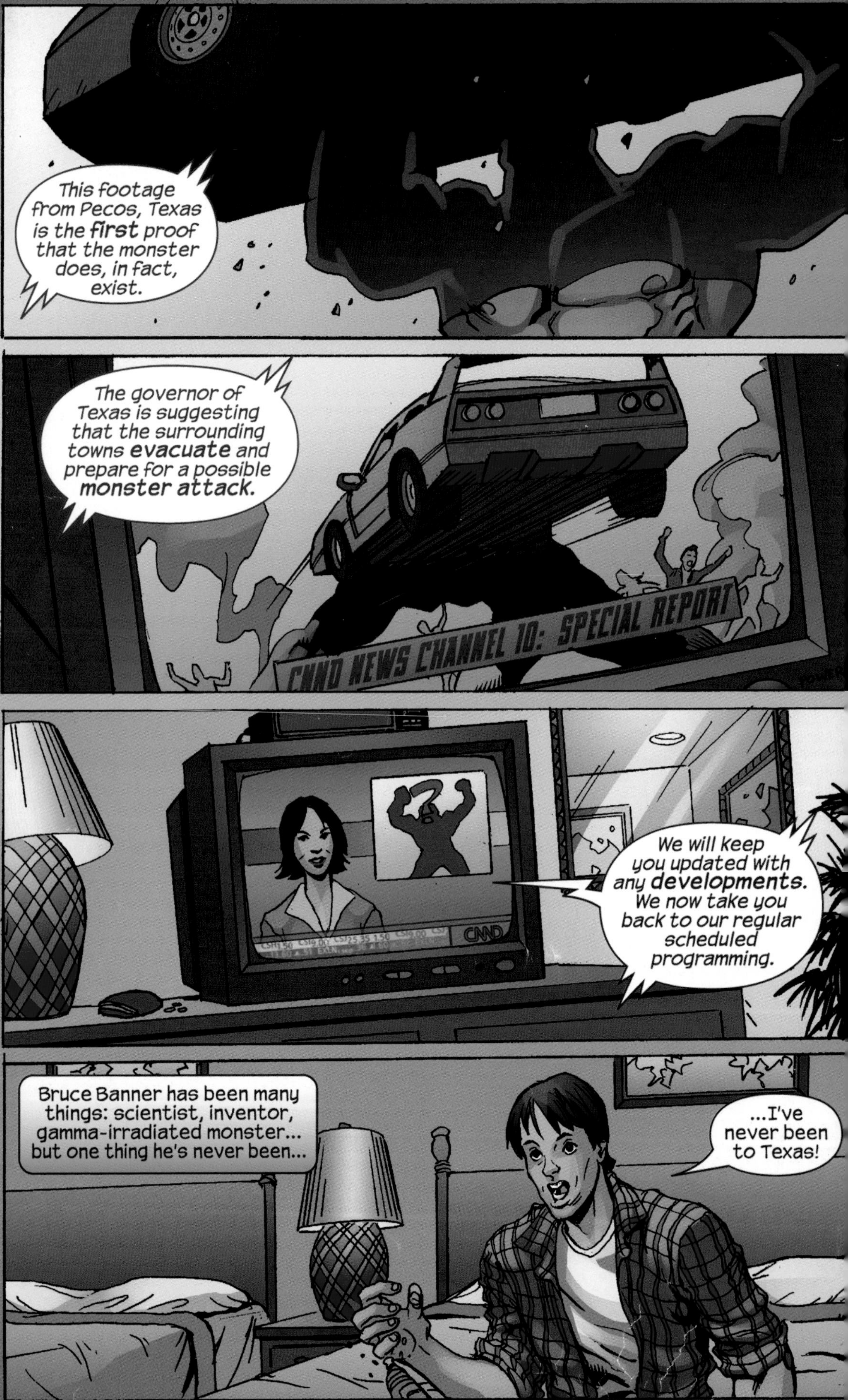
This footage from Pecos, Texas is the **first** proof that the monster does, in fact, exist.
The governor of Texas is suggesting that the surrounding towns **evacuate** and prepare for a possible **monster attack.**
CNND NEWS CHANNEL 10: SPECIAL REPORT
CNND
We will keep you updated with any **developments.** We now take you back to our regular scheduled programming.
Bruce Banner has been many things: scientist, inventor, gamma-irradiated monster... but one thing he's never been...
...I've never been to Texas!

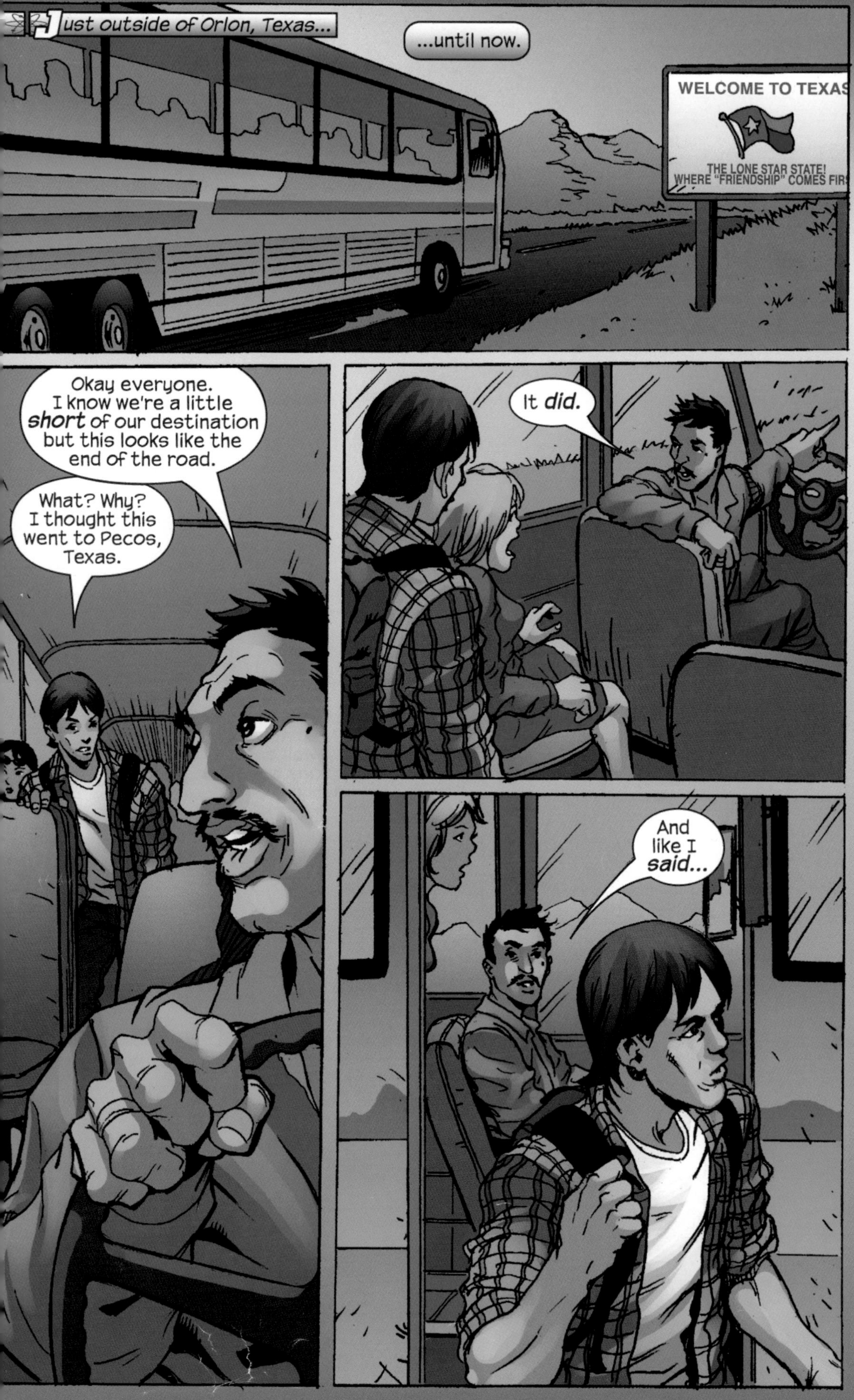
Just outside of Orlon, Texas...
...until now.
WELCOME TO TEXAS
THE LONE STAR STATE!
WHERE "FRIENDSHIP" COMES FIRS
Okay everyone. I know we're a little short of our destination but this looks like the end of the road.
What? Why? I thought this went to Pecos, Texas.
It did.
And like I said...

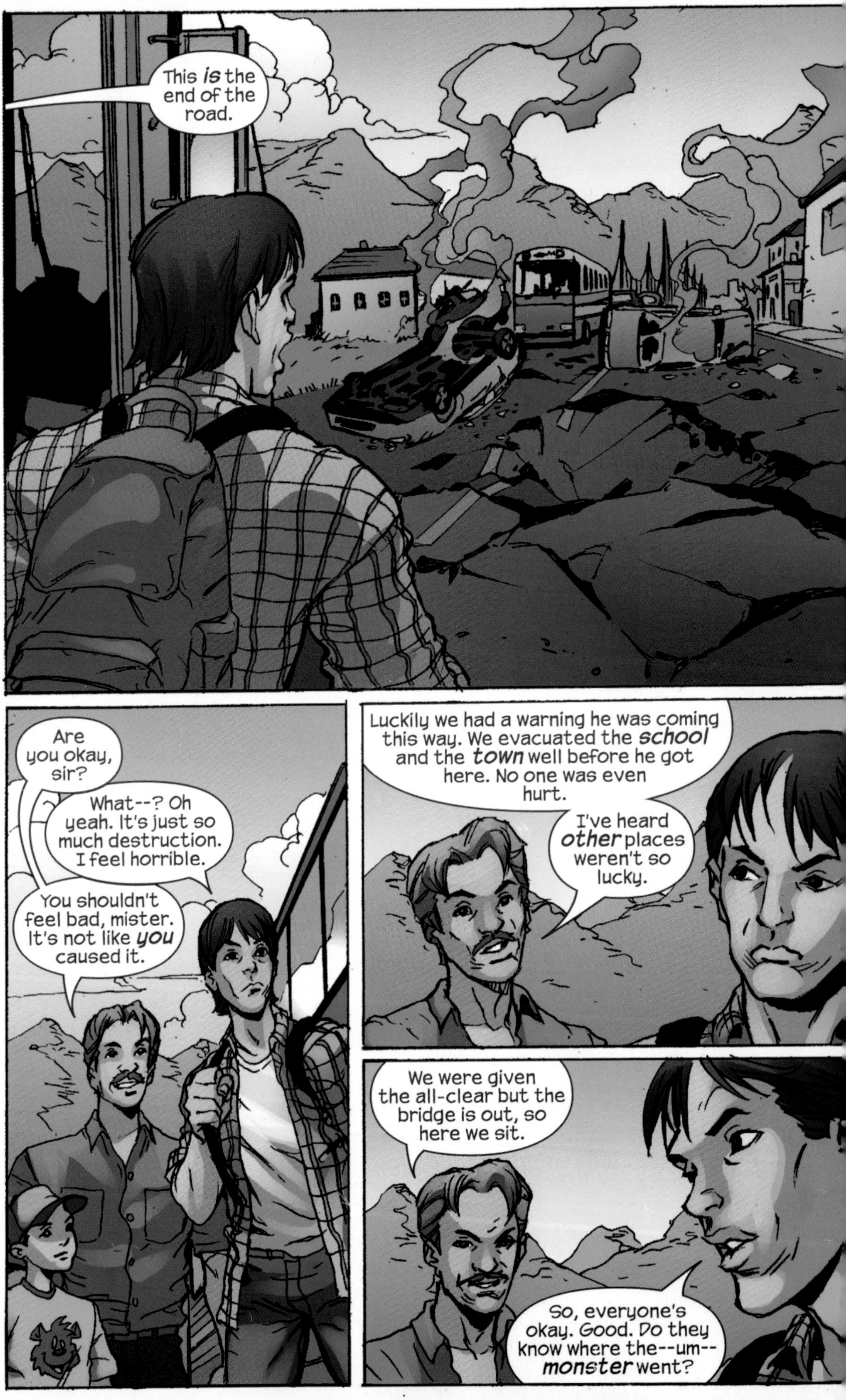
This *is* the end of the road.
Are you okay, sir?
What--? Oh yeah. It's just so much destruction. I feel horrible.
You shouldn't feel bad, mister. It's not like *you* caused it.
Luckily we had a warning he was coming this way. We evacuated the *school* and the *town* well before he got here. No one was even hurt.
I've heard *other* places weren't so lucky.
We were given the all-clear but the bridge is out, so here we sit.
So, everyone's okay. Good. Do they know where the--um--*monster* went?

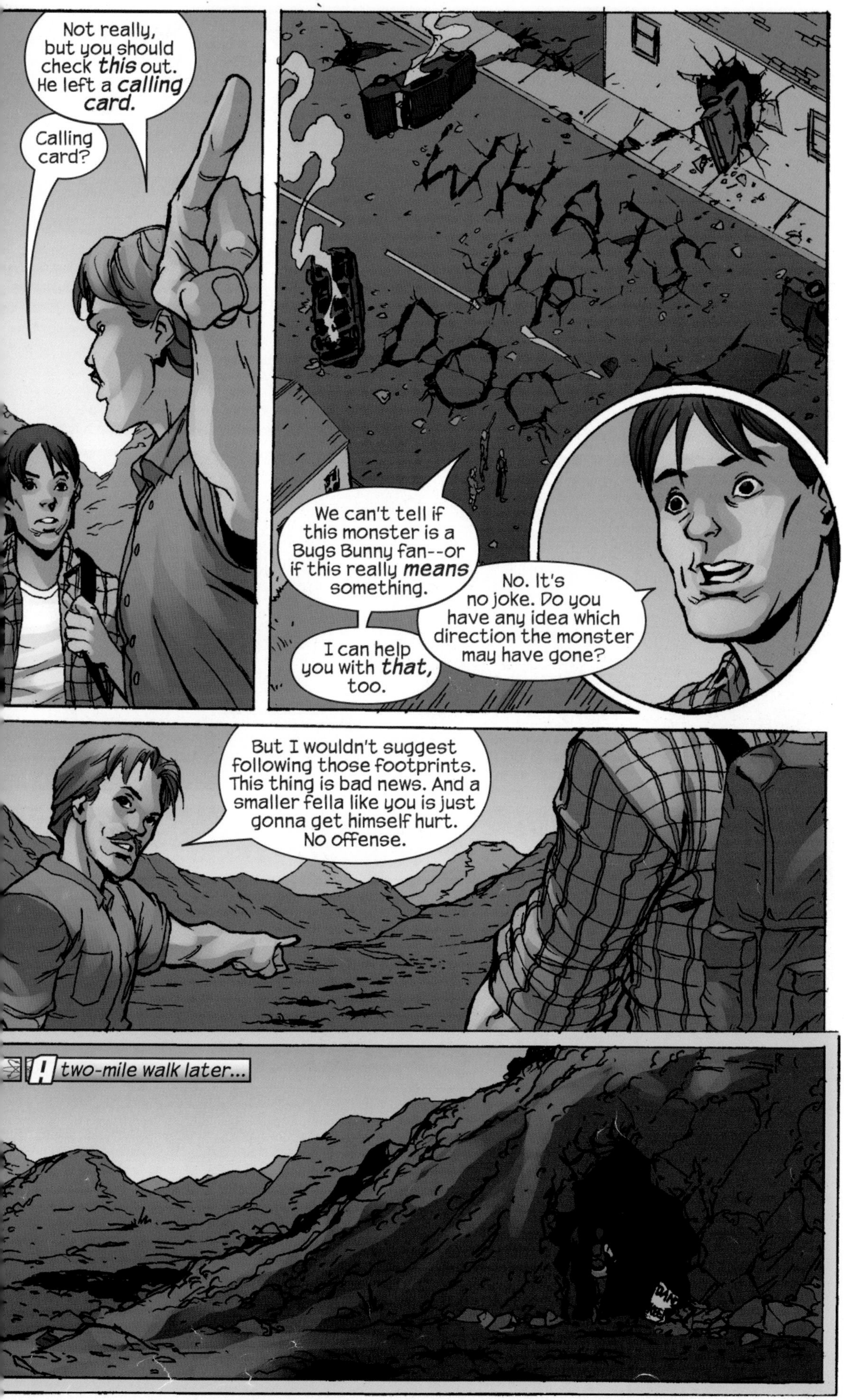

Not really, but you should check *this* out. He left a *calling card.*
Calling card?
WHAT'S UP DOC
We can't tell if this monster is a Bugs Bunny fan--or if this really *means* something.
I can help you with *that,* too.
No. It's no joke. Do you have any idea which direction the monster may have gone?
But I wouldn't suggest following those footprints. This thing is bad news. And a smaller fella like you is just gonna get himself hurt. No offense.
A two-mile walk later...

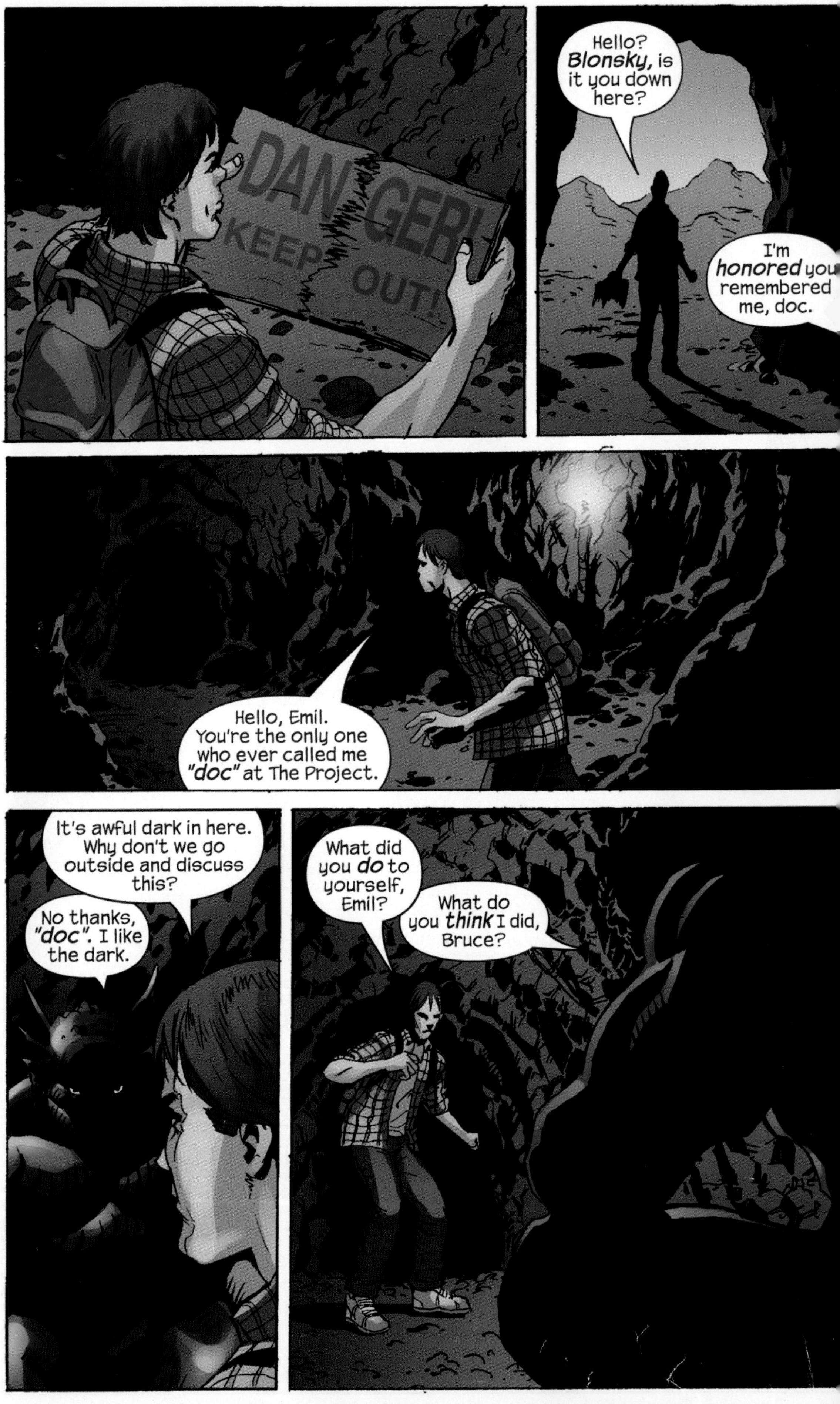
DANGER! KEEP OUT!
Hello? Blonsky, is it you down here?
I'm honored you remembered me, doc.
Hello, Emil. You're the only one who ever called me "doc" at The Project.
It's awful dark in here. Why don't we go outside and discuss this?
No thanks, "doc". I like the dark.
What did you do to yourself, Emil?
What do you think I did, Bruce?

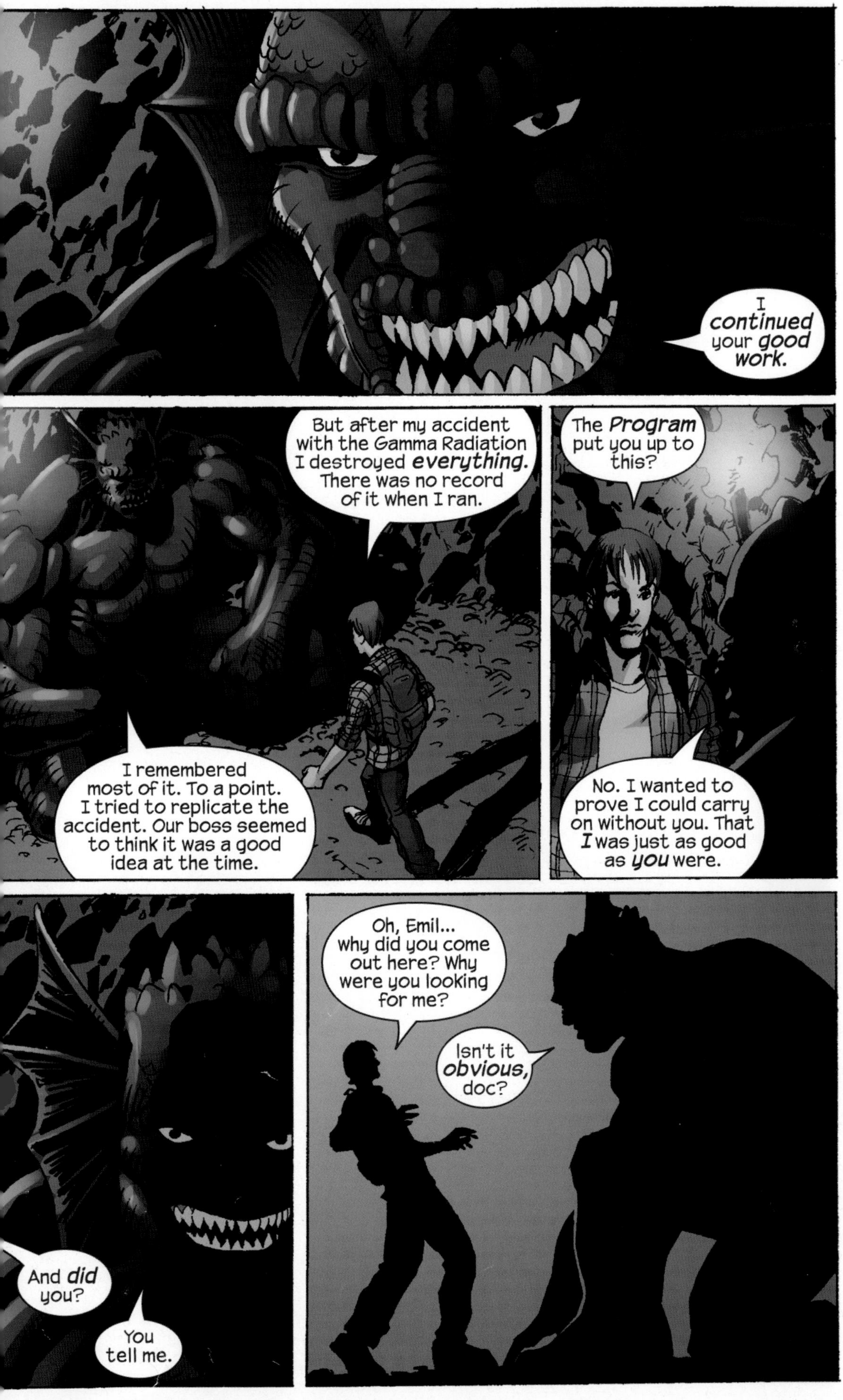

I continued your good work.
But after my accident with the Gamma Radiation I destroyed everything. There was no record of it when I ran.
I remembered most of it. To a point. I tried to replicate the accident. Our boss seemed to think it was a good idea at the time.
The Program put you up to this?
No. I wanted to prove I could carry on without you. That I was just as good as you were.
And did you?
You tell me.
Oh, Emil... why did you come out here? Why were you looking for me?
Isn't it obvious, doc?

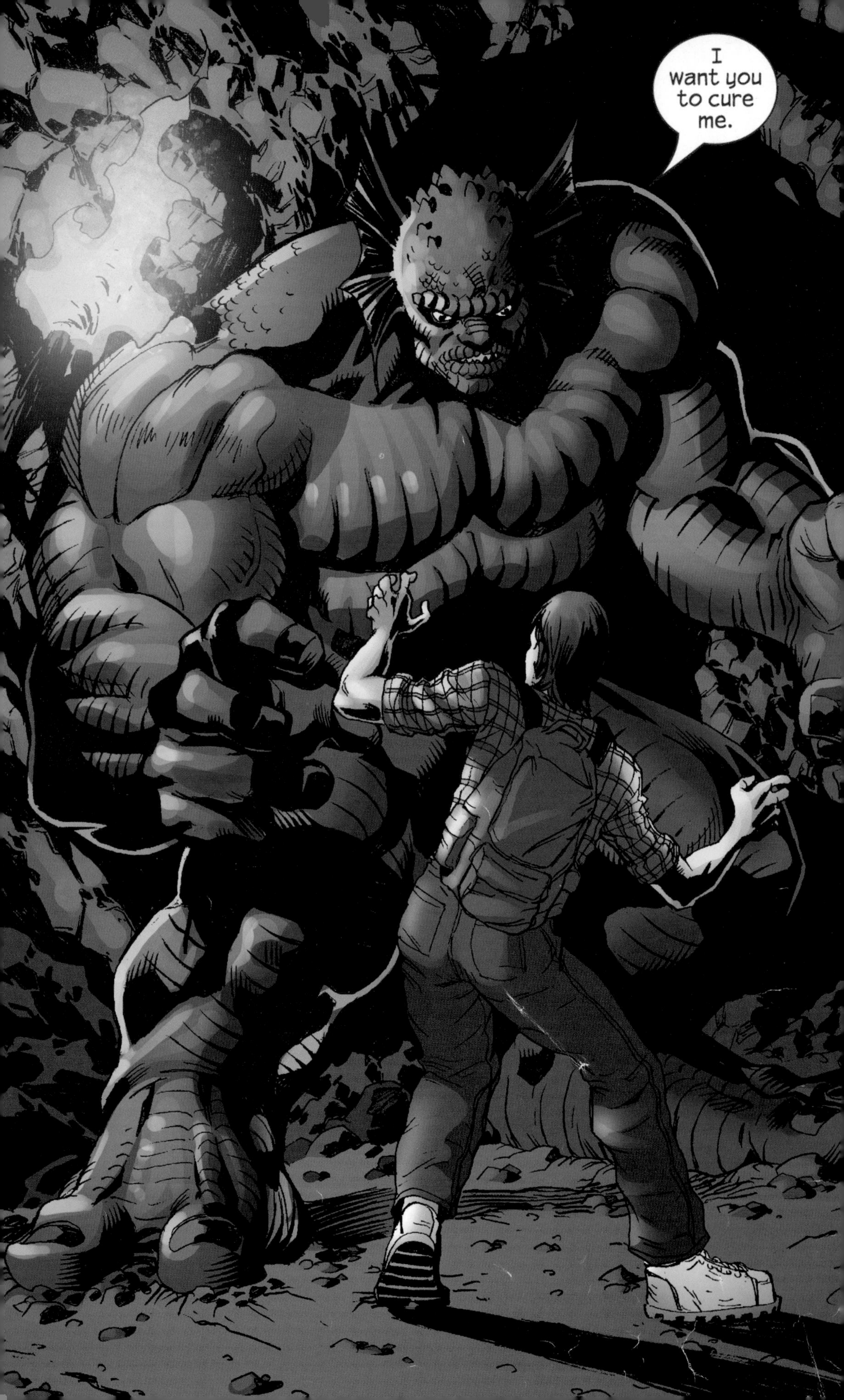
I want you to cure me.

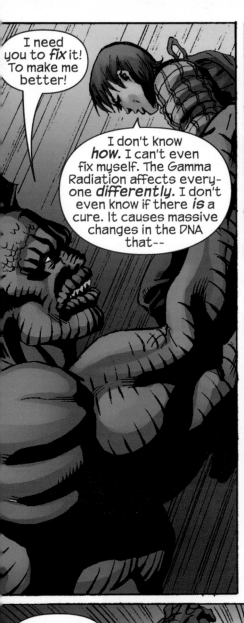

I need you to *fix* it! To make me better!

I don't know *how.* I can't even fix myself. The Gamma Radiation affects everyone *differently.* I don't even know if there *is* a cure. It causes massive changes in the DNA that--

Then how come you're in normal form now? Why can't I change back and forth?

I don't really change back and forth on a *whim.* Our exposure levels were completely different so there's no way to--

Liar!

Please, Emil. Calm down. We both need to stay calm.

I'm an abomination! A monster! Why can't I change back?

I don't know. But you have to stop acting crazy. You're a good man, Emil, but destroying cities-- endangering lives. This isn't you.

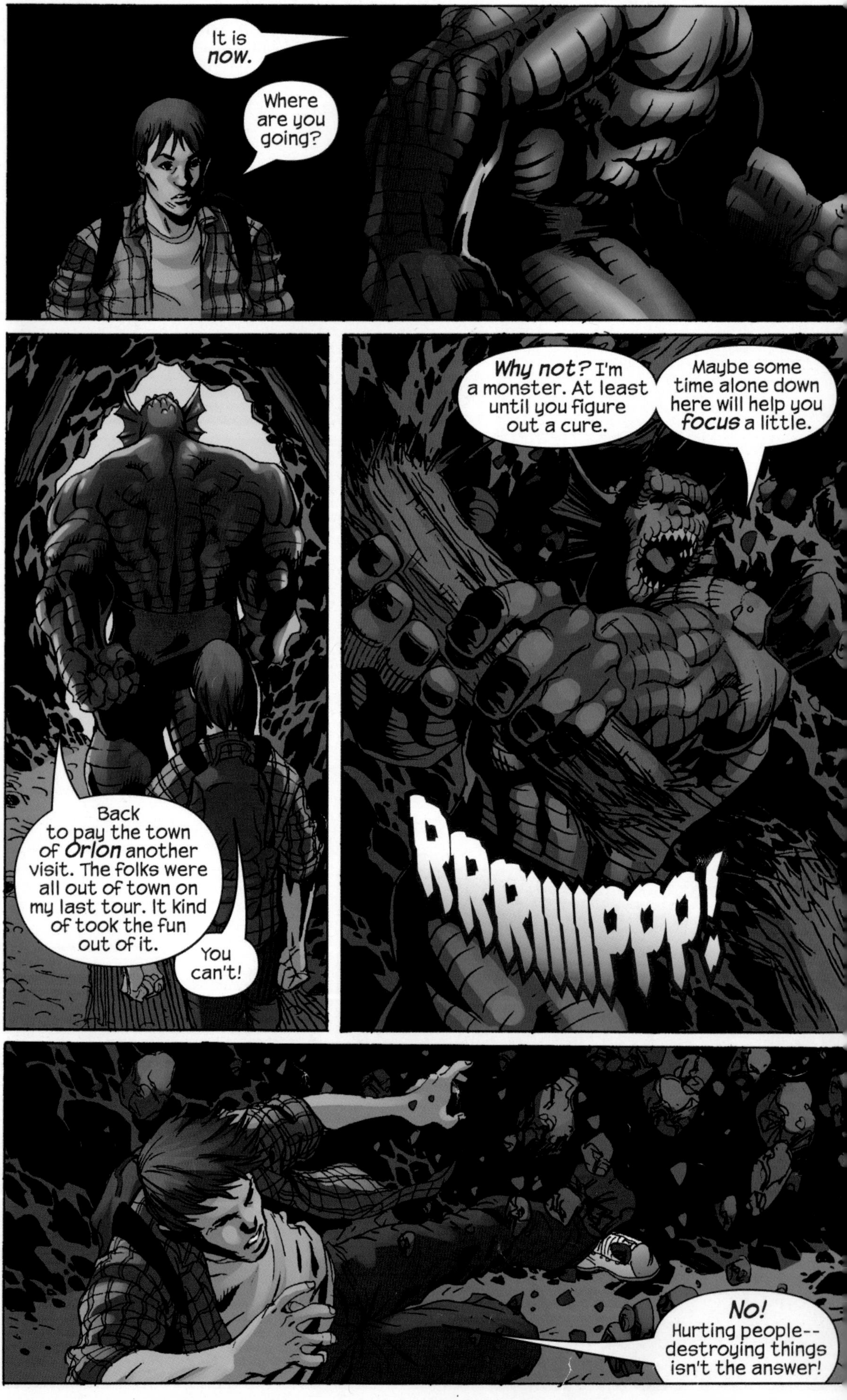
It is *now.*
Where are you going?
Back to pay the town of *Orlon* another visit. The folks were all out of town on my last tour. It kind of took the fun out of it.
You can't!
Why not? I'm a monster. At least until you figure out a cure.
Maybe some time alone down here will help you *focus* a little.
RRRIIIIPPP!
No! Hurting people--destroying things isn't the answer!

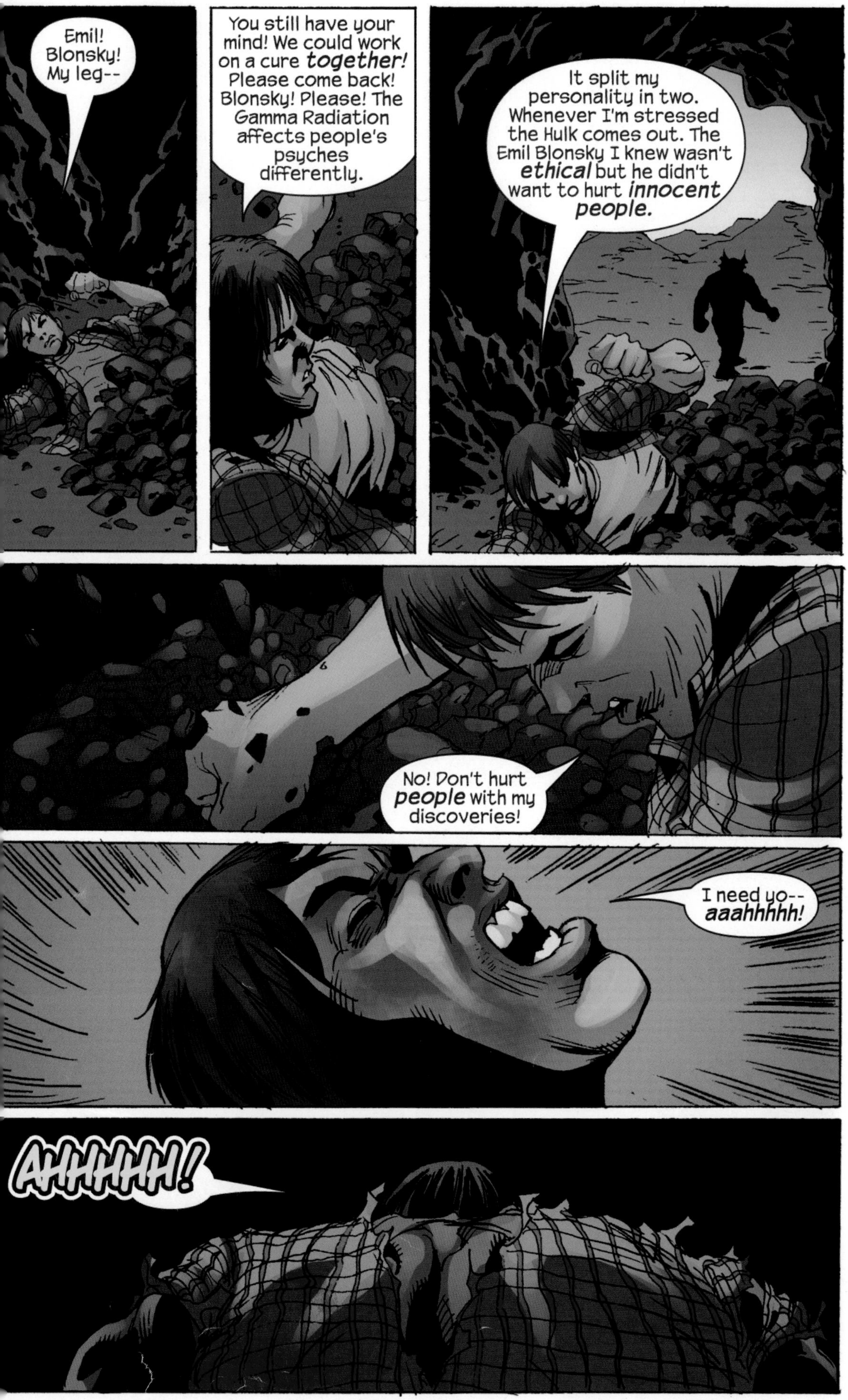
Emil! Blonsky! My leg--
You still have your mind! We could work on a cure together! Please come back! Blonsky! Please! The Gamma Radiation affects people's psyches differently.
It split my personality in two. Whenever I'm stressed the Hulk comes out. The Emil Blonsky I knew wasn't ethical but he didn't want to hurt innocent people.
No! Don't hurt people with my discoveries!
I need yo--aaahhhhh!
AHHHHH!

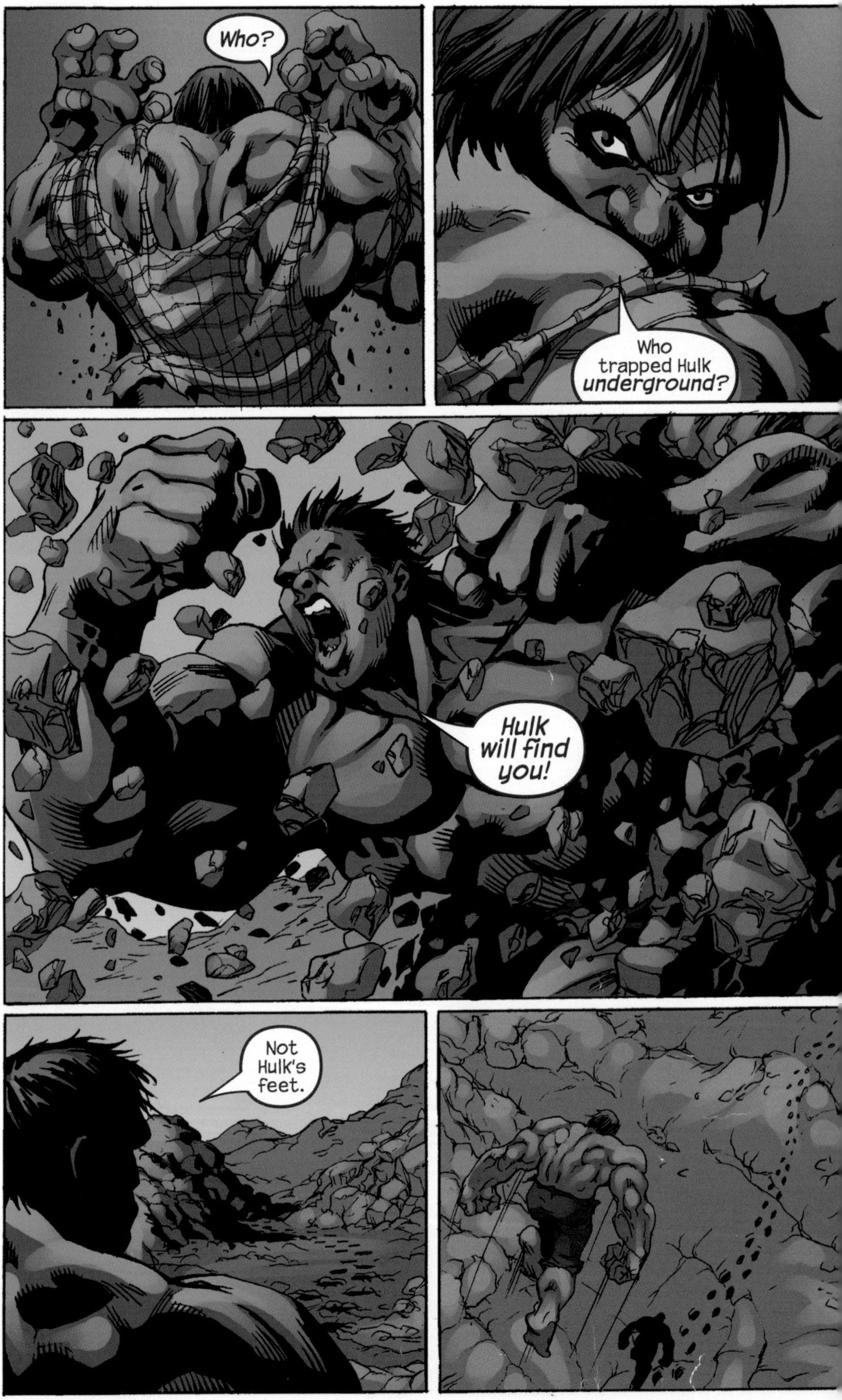
Who?
Who trapped Hulk underground?
Hulk will find you!
Not Hulk's feet.

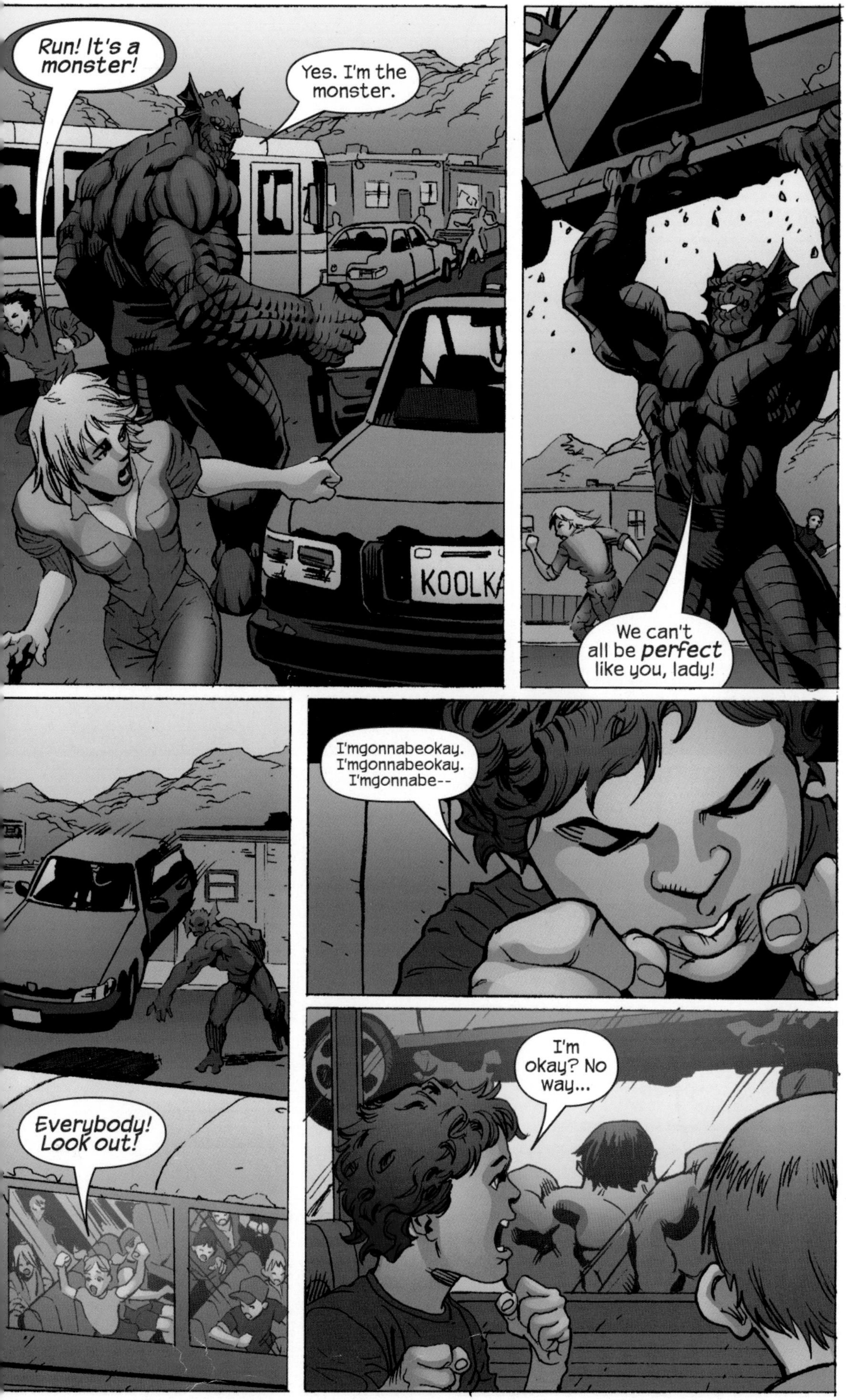

Run! It's a monster!
Yes. I'm the monster.
KOOLKA
We can't all be perfect like you, lady!
I'mgonnabeokay. I'mgonnabeokay. I'mgonnabe--
Everybody! Look out!
I'm okay? No way...

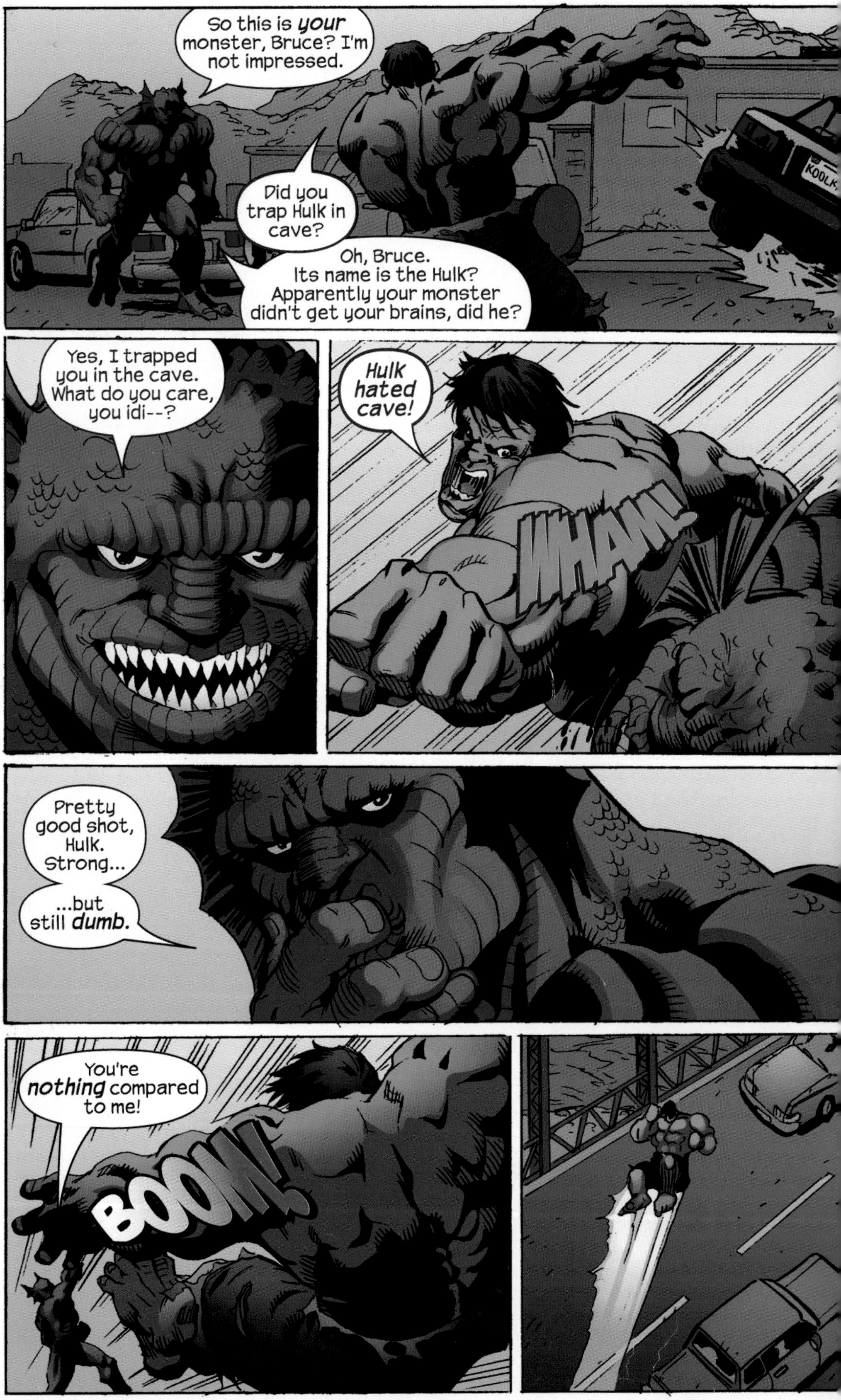
So this is your monster, Bruce? I'm not impressed.
Did you trap Hulk in cave?
Oh, Bruce. Its name is the Hulk? Apparently your monster didn't get your brains, did he?
KOOLK
Yes, I trapped you in the cave. What do you care, you idi--?
Hulk hated cave!
WHAM!
Pretty good shot, Hulk. Strong...
...but still dumb.
You're nothing compared to me!
BOOM!

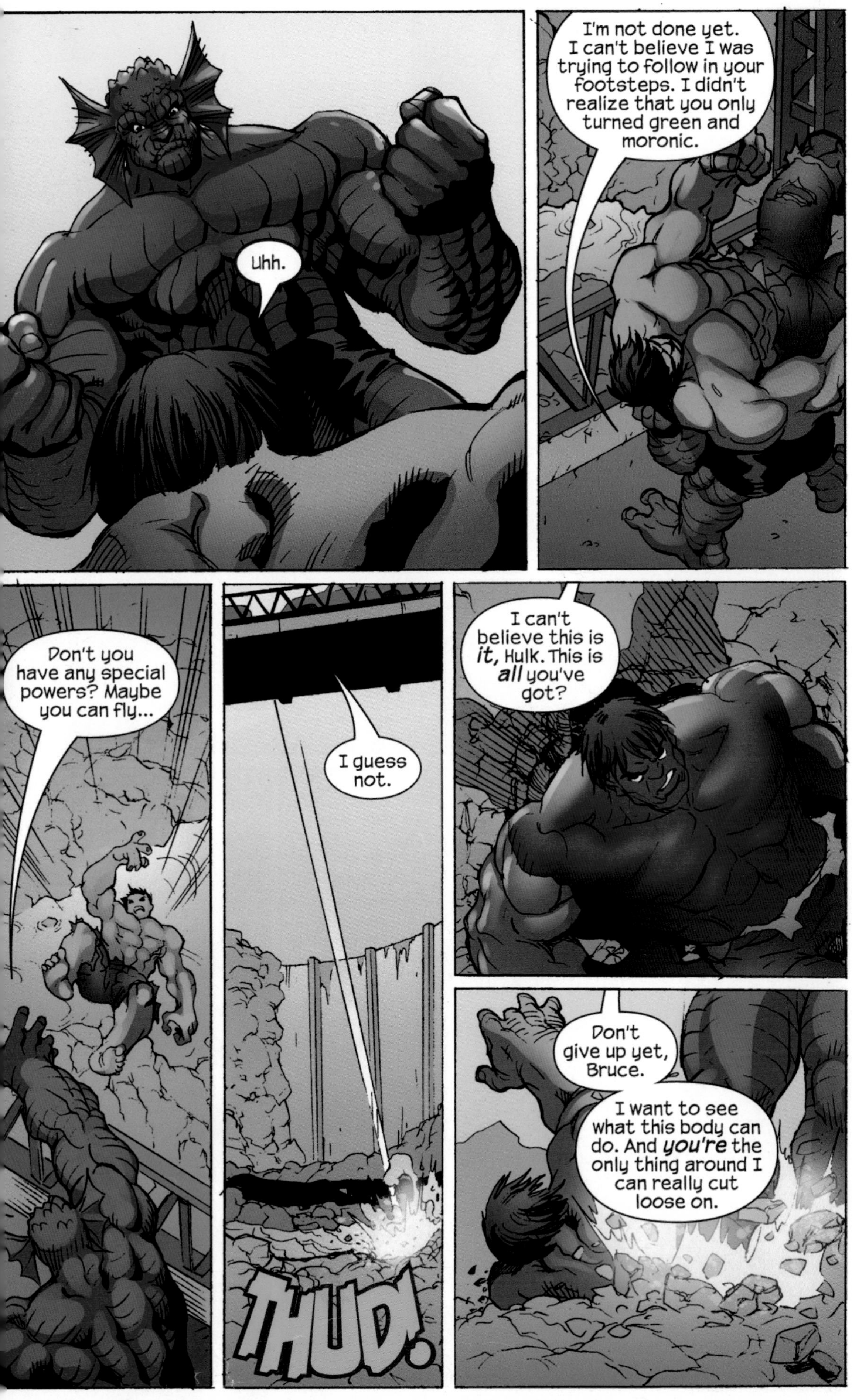
Uhh.
I'm not done yet. I can't believe I was trying to follow in your footsteps. I didn't realize that you only turned green and moronic.
Don't you have any special powers? Maybe you can fly...
I guess not.
THUD!
I can't believe this is *it,* Hulk. This is *all* you've got?
Don't give up yet, Bruce.
I want to see what this body can do. And *you're* the only thing around I can really cut loose on.

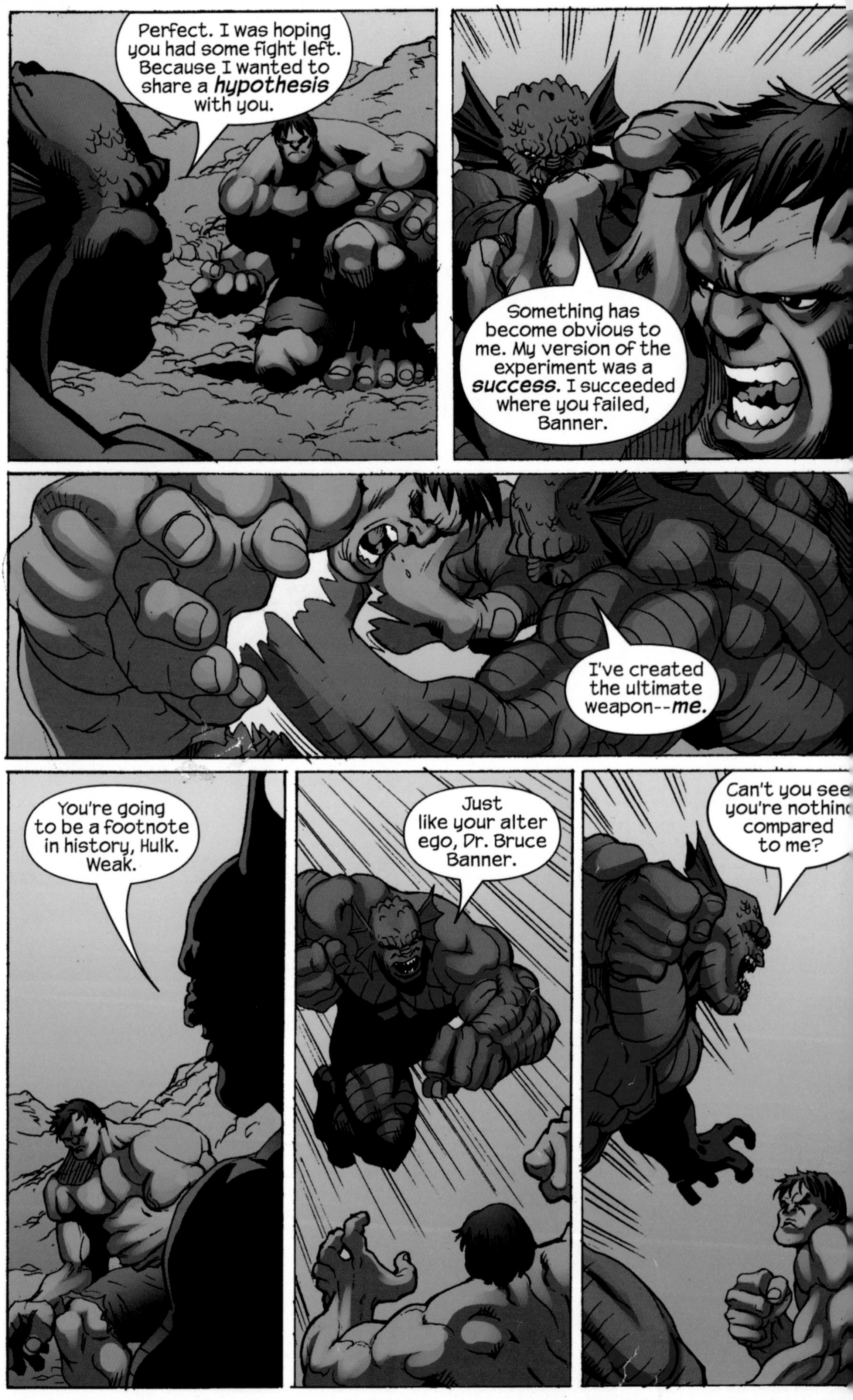
Perfect. I was hoping you had some fight left. Because I wanted to share a *hypothesis* with you.
Something has become obvious to me. My version of the experiment was a *success.* I succeeded where you failed, Banner.
I've created the ultimate weapon--*me.*
You're going to be a footnote in history, Hulk. Weak.
Just like your alter ego, Dr. Bruce Banner.
Can't you see you're nothing compared to me?

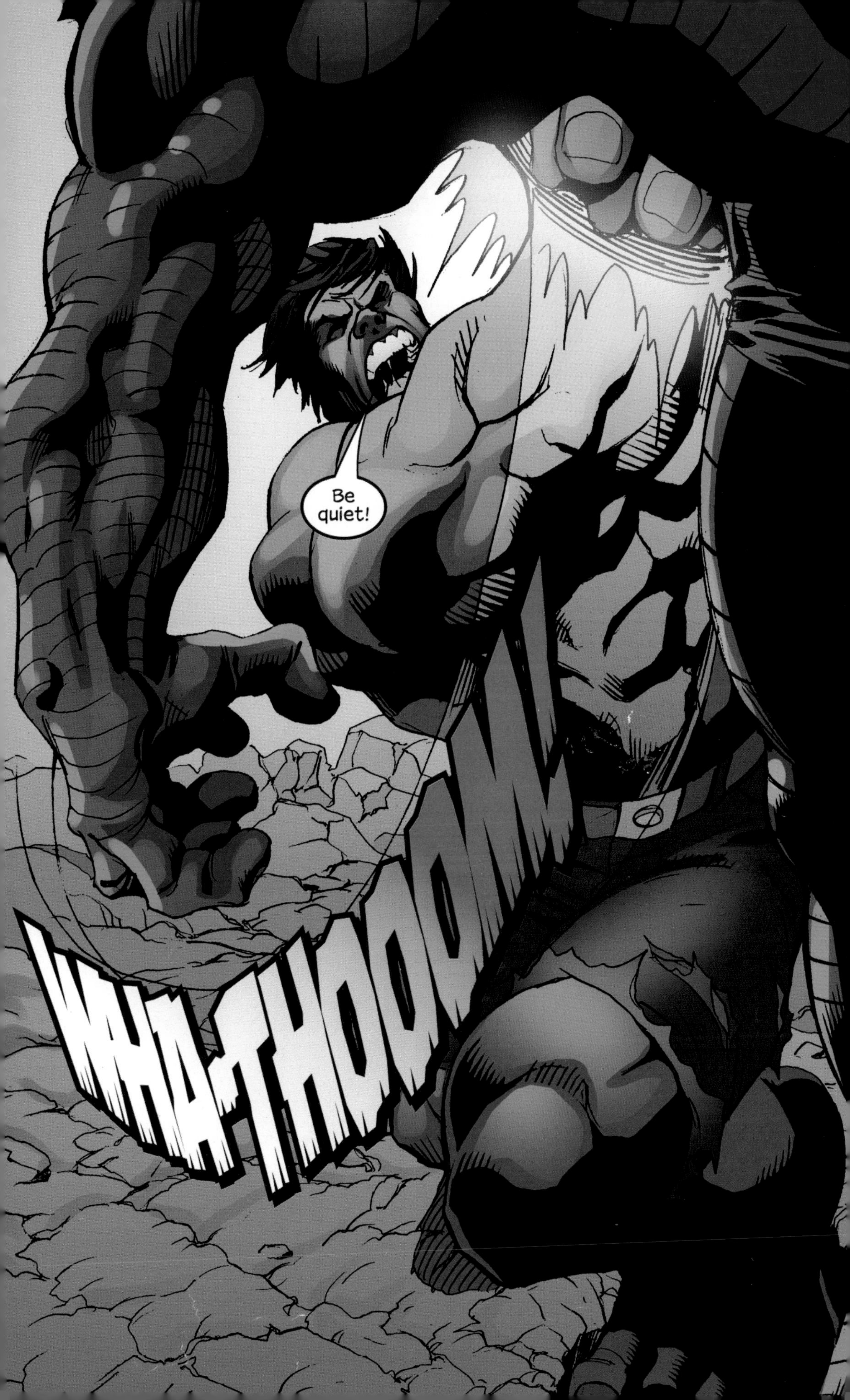
Be quiet!
WHATHOOOM

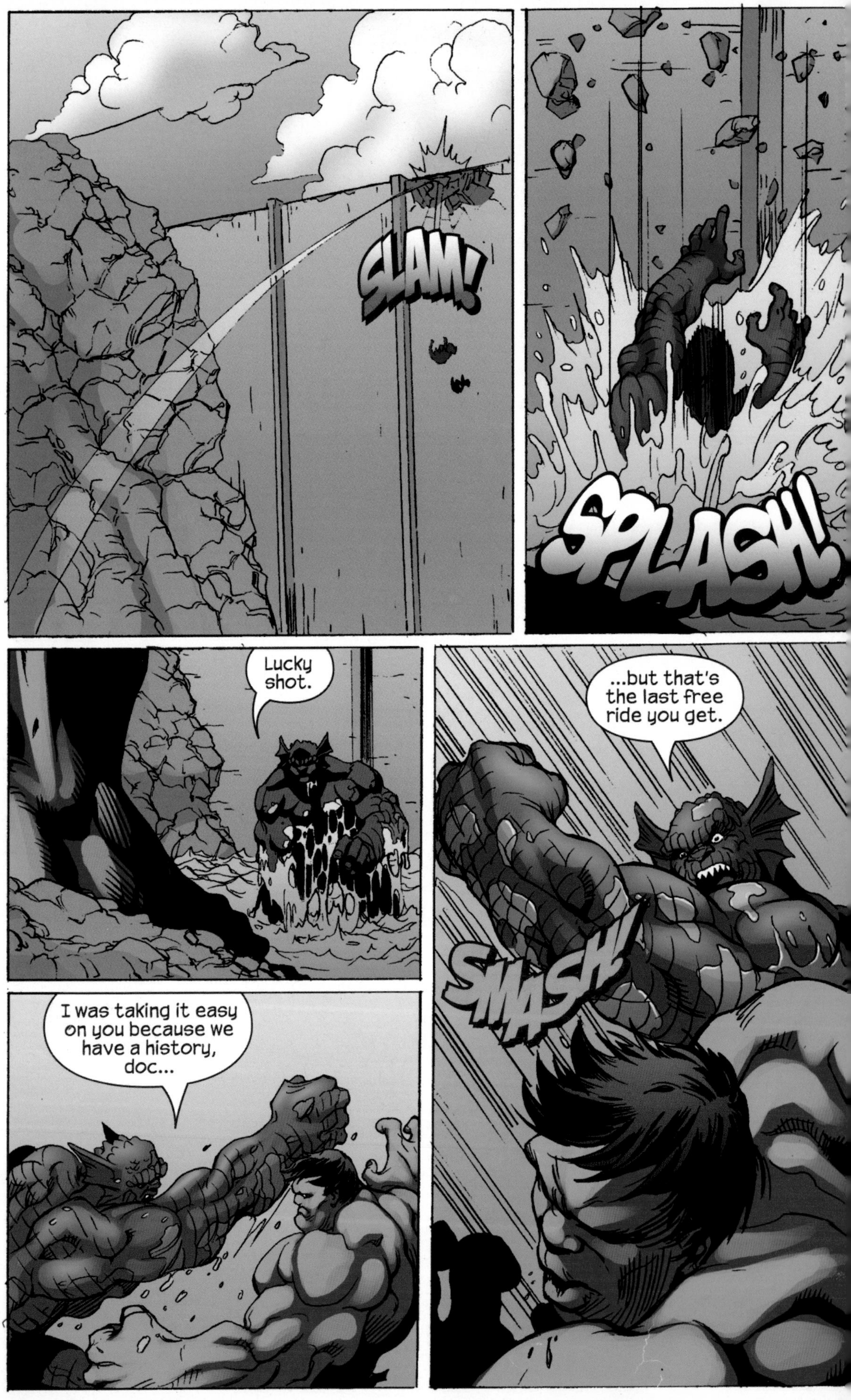
SLAM!
SPLASH!
Lucky shot.
I was taking it easy on you because we have a history, doc...
...but that's the last free ride you get.
SMASH!

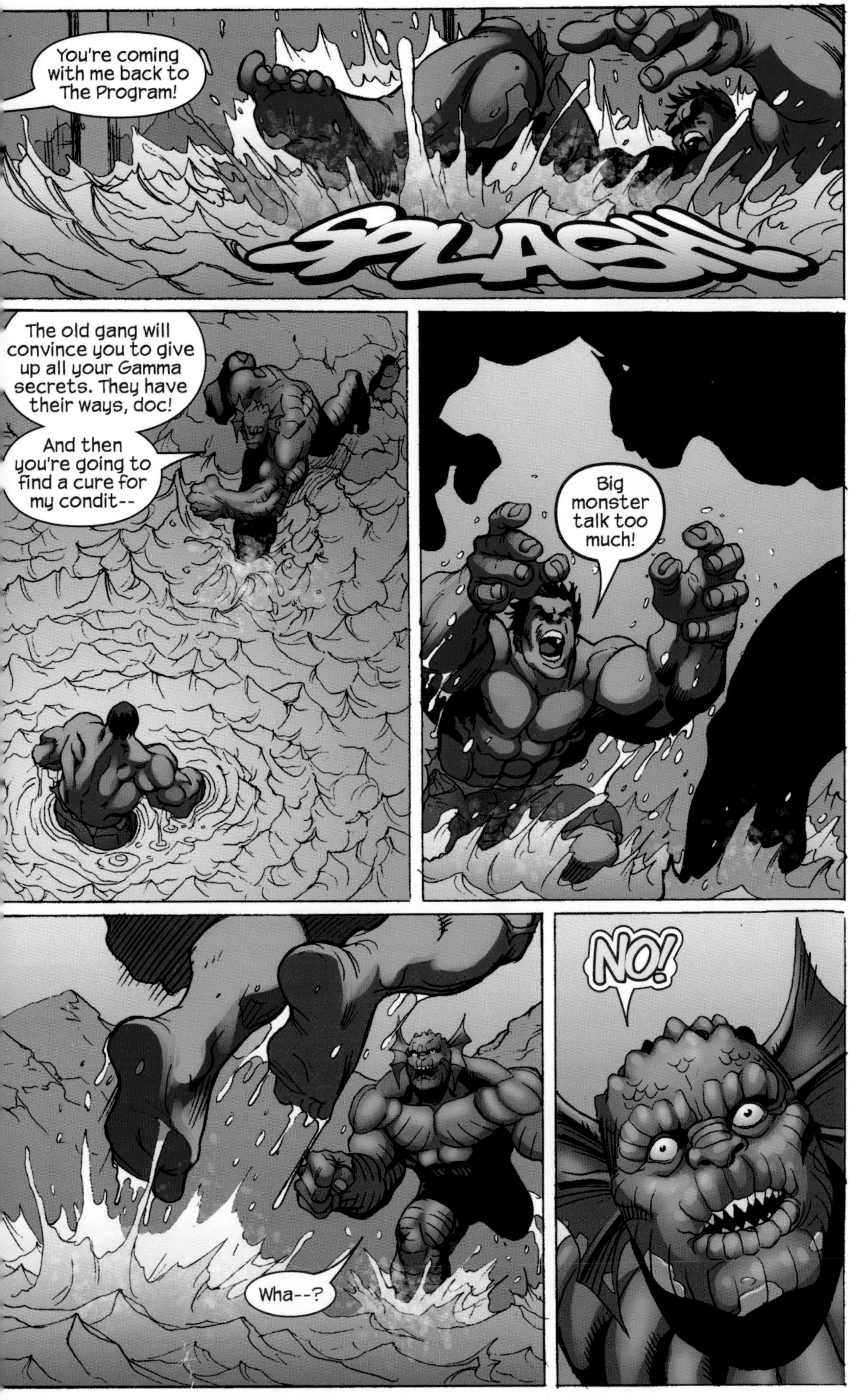
You're coming with me back to The Program!
SPLASH!
The old gang will convince you to give up all your Gamma secrets. They have their ways, doc!
And then you're going to find a cure for my condit--
Big monster talk too much!
Wha--?
NO!

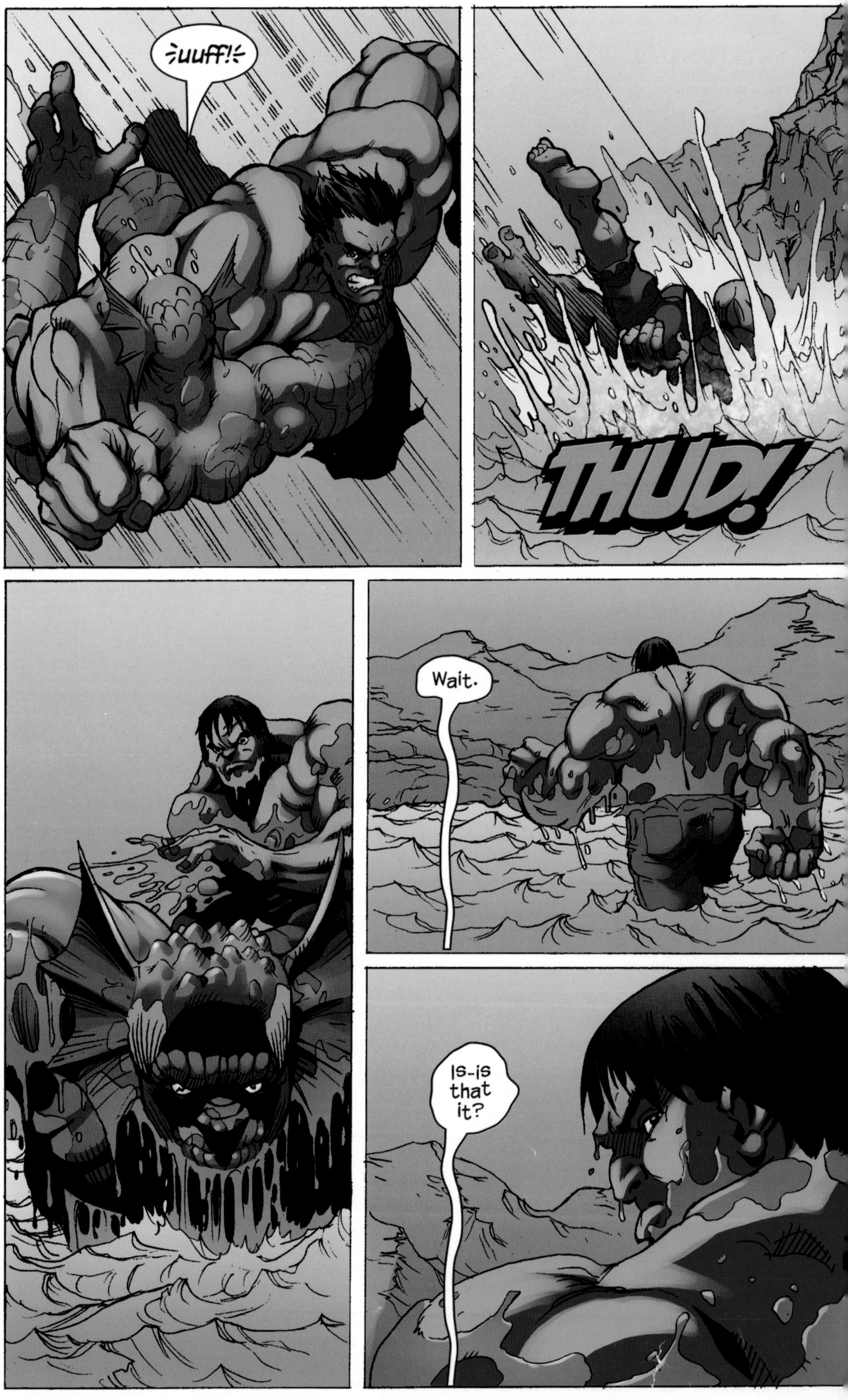

uuff!
THUD!
Wait.
Is-is that it?

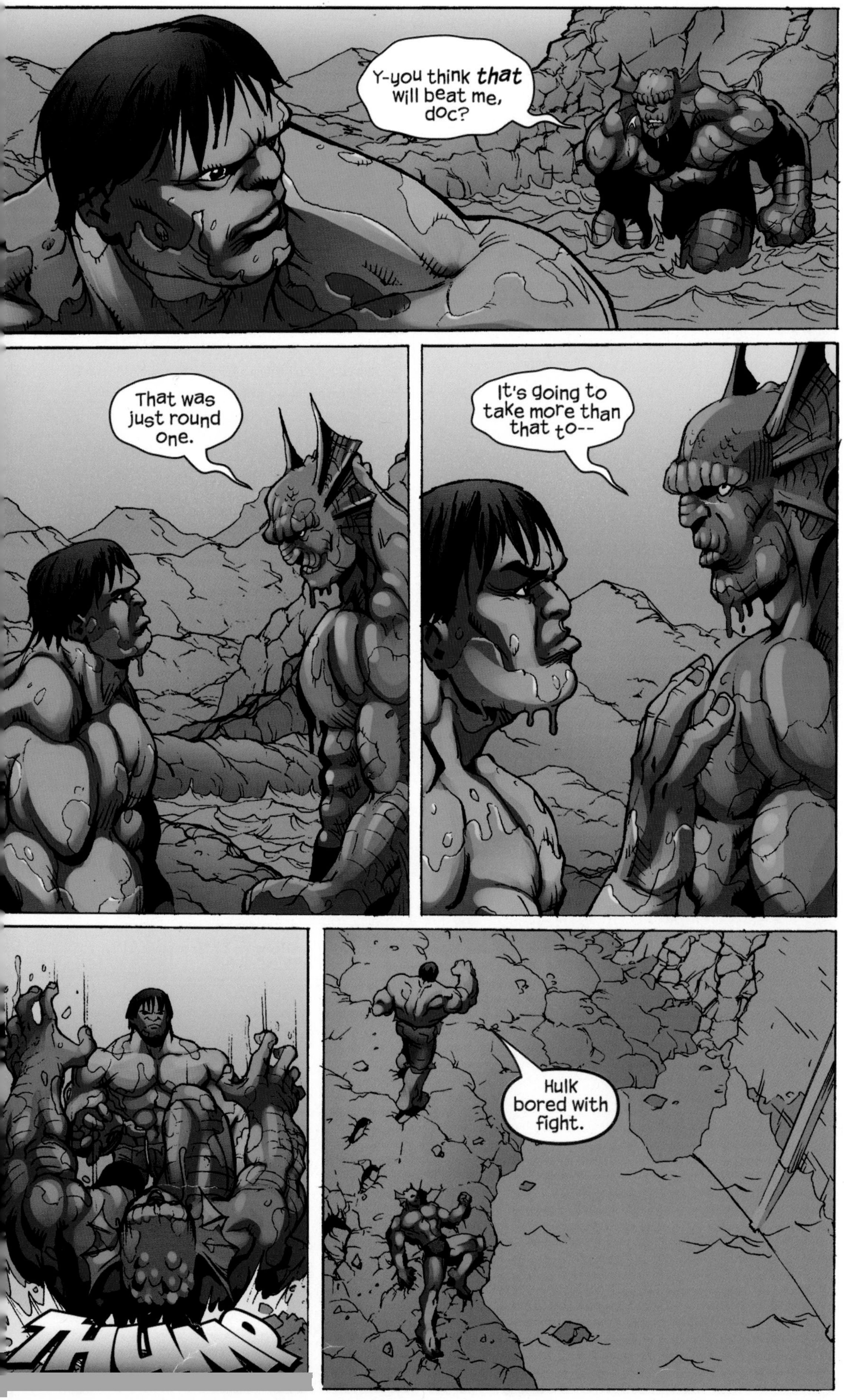
Y-you think *that* will beat me, doc?
That was just round one.
It's going to take more than that to--
THUMP
Hulk bored with fight.

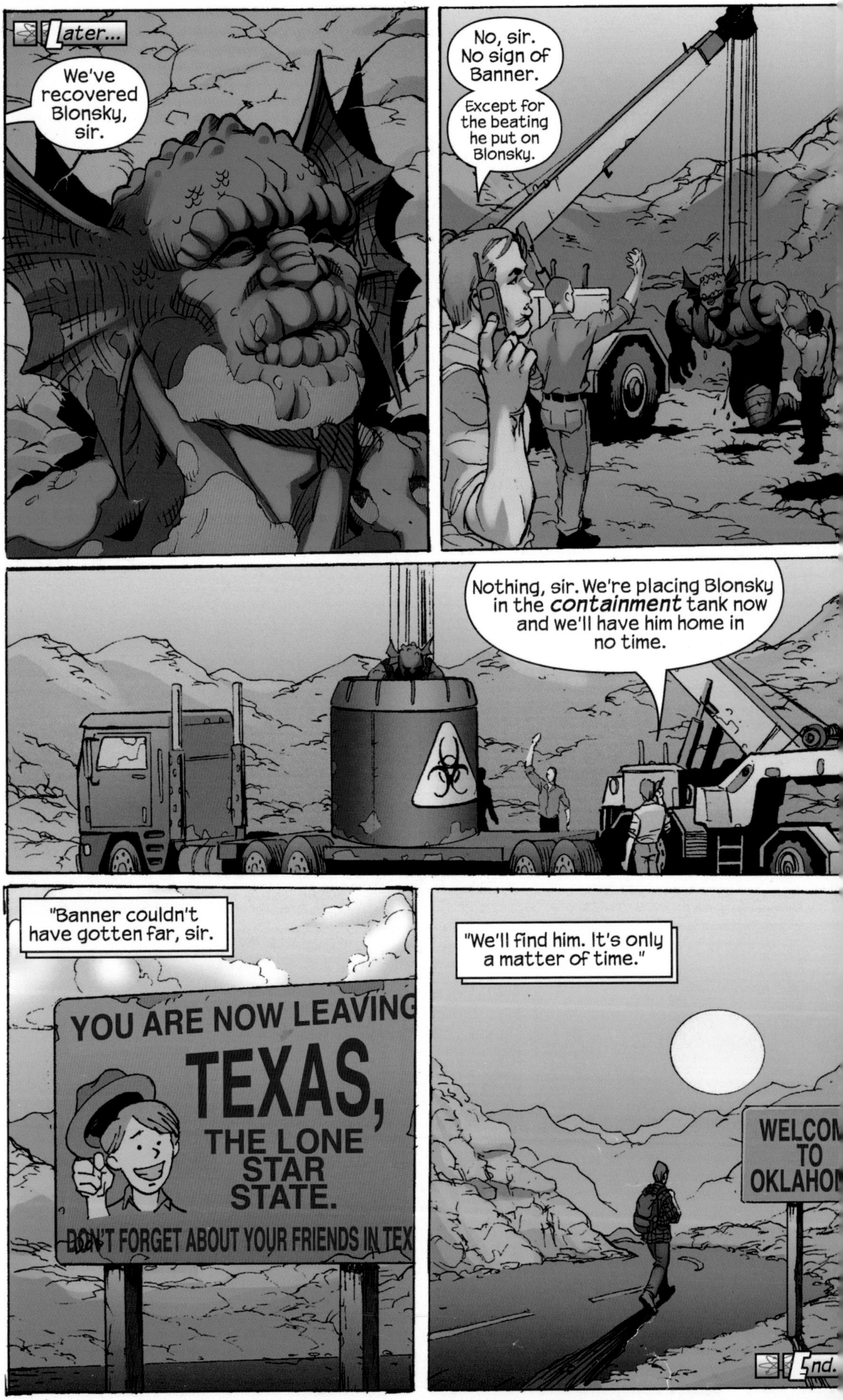
Later...
We've recovered Blonsky, sir.
No, sir. No sign of Banner.
Except for the beating he put on Blonsky.
Nothing, sir. We're placing Blonsky in the *containment* tank now and we'll have him home in no time.
"Banner couldn't have gotten far, sir.
YOU ARE NOW LEAVIN
TEXAS,
THE LONE STAR STATE.
DON'T FORGET ABOUT YOUR FRIENDS IN TEX
"We'll find him. It's only a matter of time."
WELCOM
TO
OKLAHOM
End.